HERGÉ

★

THE ADVENTURES OF
TINTIN

★

THE SECRET
OF
THE UNICORN

LITTLE, BROWN AND COMPANY
New York Boston

Little, Brown and Company

Hachette Book Group USA
237 Park Avenue, New York, NY 10017
Visit our Web site at www.lb-kids.com

Library of Congress catalog card no. 73-21250
ISBN: 978-0-316-35832-3

30 29 28 27 26 25

Published pursuant to agreement with Casterman, Paris
Not for sale in the British Commonwealth

Printed in China

THE SECRET
OF
THE UNICORN

We must keep our eyes open, and catch these crooks.

How about starting in the Old Street Market? Tintin said he was going there this morning. Perhaps we'll meet him.

Good idea. Let's go.

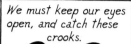

Why, there are Thomson and Thompson.

Hello! . . . How are you?

Look who's here!

Tintin!

What are you doing here? Looking for bargains?

Sh! . . . Highly confidential! . . . Special operation: pickpockets.

But that didn't stop us from finding this job-lot of walking sticks . . .

How much?

Eight bob for the lot.

Six shillings.

Seven . . . but I'm robbin' meself . . .

See? You've always got to haggle a bit here.

My wallet's been stolen!

But that's absurd! . . . You must have left it at home . . . or perhaps you've lost it?

No, I'm sure someone's stolen it!

Here, you hold these sticks. I'll pay.

Just the sort of thing that would happen to you! . . . To go and let someone pinch your wallet!

Mine's gone too!

Here, let me pay for them.

Thanks very much, Tintin. We'll pay you back tomorrow.

There.

Goodbye! We're going to report this straight away . . .

Stop thief! . . . Help! . . . My suitcase! . . .

What's going on?

They caught some thieves red-handed.

Special Branch! Special Branch! . . . You can tell that to the Inspector!

Snowy! . . . Snowy!

All right, I'm coming . . .

I say, Snowy, isn't that a fine ship!

It really is a beauty. I've a good mind to buy it for Captain Haddock . . .

How much?

A quid. It's a unique specimen. It's a very old . . . er . . . very old type of galliard.

Seventeen and six!

Done! Yours for seventeen and six.

How much is that ship?

Sorry, sir. I just sold it to this young gent.

!

I'll buy it from you.

I'm sorry, sir, but it's not for sale.

Look here, young fellow, I'm a collector . . . How much did you pay? I'll give you double for it!

Thanks, but I'm keeping it.

How much is that ship?

I'm sorry, sir, but this ship is not for sale.

Look. I'll give you a fiver for it!

A tenner!

NO!

Twenty!

Thirty!

Look here: I want to give this ship to a friend of mine. I'm not selling it, so please don't pester me any more!

Now why were they both so keen to buy my ship?

A few minutes later . . .

It really is superb . . . Captain Haddock will be delighted.

RRRING

I expect that's him . . .

I apologise: it's me again!

?

Forgive me if I am too insistent. But as I explained, I'm a collector - a collector of model ships. And I would be so very grateful if you would agree to sell me your ship.

I've already told you, I bought it for a friend . . .

Exactly! Now I have other ships just as good as yours, and we could exchange them so that your friend . . .

It's no good. Please don't go on. I'm keeping it.

Very well. But think it over. I'll give you my card, so that if you change your mind . . .

I shouldn't count on it!

Well, I shall hope.

Goodbye, sir.

?

CRASH

What's happened?

Snowy! . . . What have you done?

Look, now it's broken!

Luckily it's not too bad. I can soon mend it.

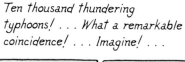

RRRRING

This time it must be the Captain.

Hello!

Hello, Captain. Just the person I wanted to see.

Come on in. I've got a surprise for you.

Tintin, what a magnificent ship!

Thundering typhoons!

Where . . . where did you find this ship?

In the Old Street Market . . . Why?

Ten thousand thundering typhoons! . . . What a remarkable coincidence! . . . Imagine! . . .

No! Come with me: then you'll see!

Remarkable! . . . It's really remarkable!

Here we are! Now . . .

You'll see . . .

Look!

Is . . . is that you? . . .

No, it's one of my ancestors, Sir Francis Haddock. He lived in the reign of Charles the Second.

But just take a closer look at that ship in the background . . .

It's just like the one you saw in my room, isn't it?

Exactly! . . . It's the same ship! . . . It's identical! . . . Don't you think that's remarkable?

There's a name here. Look there, in tiny letters: UNICORN.

So there is: UNICORN. I'd never noticed it.

Maybe there's a name on mine too . . . We should have brought it along. Wait here: I'll go and fetch it.

If mine has the same name, that'll really be funny . . .

Let's see . . .

Great snakes! . . . It's gone!

RRRING . . .
RRRING . . .
RRRING . . .

Hello? . . . Yes . . . Ah, it's you . . . Well, has your ship got the same name? . . . What did you say? . . . It's been stolen?

Yes, stolen! . . . Do I suspect anybody? No one at all . . . at least . . . Look Captain, I'll ring you again later . . .

Yes . . . he's the only possibility . . .

IVAN IVANOVITCH SAKHARINE
Collector
21, Eucalyptus Avenue

Just you wait, Mr Ivan Ivanovitch Sakharine!

Here we are . . .

I've a hunch that we're off on one of our adventures again . . .

EUCALYPTUS AVENUE

RRRING

21

Something tells me he's going to get a surprise when he opens the door!

Ah, there you are! . . . Come in . . . I was expecting you.

!

What? . . . Expecting me? . . . Then you know why I've come.

But of course . . .

You've come to tell me that you'll sell your ship after all . . .

Certainly not!

No? . . . Then I don't understand . . .

Is this where you keep your collection? . . . I've come to tell you, sir . . . that my ship has been stolen . . .

. . . and that I'm waiting for you to explain how it comes to be here!

You are mistaken, young man. I've had this ship for more than ten years! . . .

Ten years? But you were trying to buy it from me less than two hours ago!

This wasn't the ship! . . . Not this one! . . . Yours was, in fact, exactly the same, but it wasn't this one!

Indeed? . . .

Well, sir, we can soon tell. Just after you'd gone, my ship fell over and the mainmast was broken. I put it back, but you can see where it broke. So we'll look at your mainmast, if you don't mind!

It's not broken! . . . This isn't my ship!

So, you see!

I can understand your surprise. I myself was amazed to find an exact replica of my own vessel in the Old Street Market. And because it seemed so odd, I did all I could to persuade you to part with it . . .

UNICORN

Please do forgive me, sir . . . I am so very sorry . . .

That's all right! And if you find your ship, let me know.

It's extremely odd! Two ships exactly like the one in the Captain's picture . . . and with the same name: UNICORN.

I must telephone the Captain at once: He'll be amazed!

Engaged!

It really is unbelievable how long people can chatter on the telephone! More than a quarter of an hour! Ah, at last!

We can go now, Fifi: it has stopped raining . . .

No reply: the Captain must have gone out. We'll go home . . .

As for my burglar, it must have been the second man who tried to buy the ship . . .

My door's open! . . . What can be the matter now? . . .

My flat has been ransacked! . . .

The gangsters! What have they done to my books?

This one is completely ruined! . . . The vandals!

Burgled twice in one day . . . Not bad at all!

What have they taken this time?

Very queer thieves: they haven't taken a thing.

They've only searched the place . . . I wonder what they were looking for? . . .

Next morning . . .

9

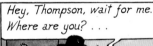

Poor old Thomsons, they do have rotten luck! . . . There seems to be quite an epidemic of larceny and house-breaking.

Oh well, let's try and get these papers sorted out . . .

What are you after, Snowy?

A cigarette, under there? That's a funny place . . .

Why, it's not a cigarette . . . it's a little scroll of parchment . . .

But this isn't mine! Where ever did it come from? . . . Let's have a closer look at it . . .

Here's another mystery!

Three Brothers joyned. Three Vnicornes in company sailing in the noonday Sunne will speak. For 'tis from the Light that Light will Dawn. And then shines forth the Eagle's †

42   1

But it's all gibberish! And where on earth did this parchment come from, anyway?

Great snakes! I've got it . . . This parchment must have been rolled up inside the mast of the ship. It fell out when the mast was broken, and it rolled under the chest . . .

And that explains something else! . . . Whoever stole my ship knew that the parchment was hidden there. When he discovered the scroll had gone, he thought I must have found it. That's why the thief came back and searched my flat, never guessing the parchment was under the chest . . .

Tintin, you're a real Sherlock Holmes!

But why was he so anxious to get hold of it? If only it made some sense . . . then at least . . .

I wonder . . . But . . . of course! . . . That must be it! There's no other answer.

Quick, Snowy! . . . We must see the Captain.

Why? What is it now?

Treasure, Snowy! . . . Come on, this is going to be a treasure-hunt!

RRRRING RRRING RRRING

HADDOCK

Yes, I'm absolutely certain it must be treasure . . .

The old lazybones! He's still in bed!

No? . . . then where can he be?

No one at home. Perhaps he's gone out. I'll ask his landlady . . .

Captain Haddock? . . . No, I didn't see him go out. Hasn't he answered the bell? That's funny . . .

Perhaps he's ill?

Ill? He might be . . . His light's been on all night . . .

We must find out at once.

RRRRRRRRING

No answer? . . .

Wait! . . . He must be in. I can hear a noise . . .

Avast, pirates! Avast there!
Captain! . . .

Avast, you dogs! . . . Sea-gherkins! . . . Baboons!

Buccaneers! . . . Fili-busters! . . . Bagpipers! . . . Gallows-fodder!

We've won! . . . That's got them on the run! . . . With a yo-ho-ho and a bottle of rum!
What's all this play-acting for?

Play-acting? . . . This isn't a play! . . . Come in, and you'll understand . . .

You see that man?
Yes, he's one of your ancestors. What about it?

Well, last night, when I was thinking about this strange business of the ships, I suddenly remembered that up in the attic I had an old sea-chest belonging to my ancestor. This is it . . .

In the chest I found this hat and cutlass, and also . . .
I know! Treasure! . . . Or a treasure-map!

No, not treasure, but something like it! . . . Old manuscripts by Sir Francis Haddock . . . Look, I started reading them yester-day evening, and read all night . . .

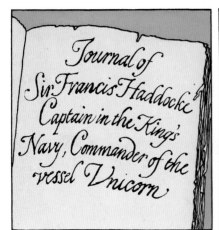
Journal of Sir Francis Haddocke Captain in the King's Navy, Commander of the vessel Unicorn

I was still reading when you came in. That's why you found me a little . . . over-excited. But what a story! Just listen to it!

It is the year 1676. The UNICORN, a valiant ship of King Charles II's fleet, has left Barbados in the West Indies, and set sail for home. She carries a cargo of . . . well, anyway, there's a good deal of rum aboard...

Two days at sea, a good stiff breeze, and the *UNICORN* is reaching on the starboard tack. Suddenly there's a hail aloft . . .

Sail on the port bow!

Thundering typhoons! . . . She's mighty close-hauled! Ration my rum if she's not going to cut across our bows!

And she's making a spanking pace! Oho! She's running up her colours . . . Now we'll see . . .

!

The Jolly Roger! Pirates! ...

Ahoy there! ... Clear the decks for action! ... Man the poop! ... Stand by to haul the wind!

Turning on to the wind with all sails set, risking her masts, the UNICORN tries to outsail the dreaded Barbary buccaneers ...

Thundering typhoons! It's no use ... She's overhauling us fast!

They must outwit the pirates. The Captain makes a daring plan. He'll wear ship, then pay off on the port tack. As the UNICORN comes abreast of the pirate he'll loose off a broadside ... No sooner said than done! ...

Ready about! ... Let go braces! ... Beat gunners to quarters!

The UNICORN has gybed completely round. Taken by surprise, the pirates have no time to alter course. The royal ship bears down upon them ... Steady ...

FIRE!

Got her!

Got her, yes! But not a crippling blow. The pirate ship in turn goes about - and look! She's hoisted fresh colours to the mast-head!

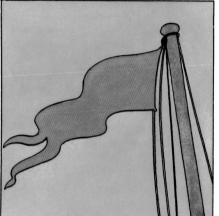

The red pennant! . . . No quarter given! . . . A fight to the death, no prisoners taken! You understand? If we're beaten, then it's every man to Davy Jones's locker!

The pirates take up the chase - they draw closer . . . and closer . . . Throats are dry aboard the UNICORN.

Close hauled, the enemy falls in line astern with the UNICORN, avoiding the fire of her guns . . . She draws closer . . .

Then suddenly, not more than half a cable's length away, she slips from under the UNICORN's poop . . . whoosh, like that!

Then she resumes her course. The two ships are now alongside. The boarders prepare for action . . .

Here they come! Grappling irons are hurled from the enemy ship. With hideous yells the pirates stream aboard the *UNICORN*.

All hands to *repel boarders!*

Stand back! Out of my way! Can't you see the pirates swarming over the side!

Back, you dogs!

Back, you rats! Avast, sea-lice! Belay, lubberly scum!

Leave this man to me, lads; I want him to myself!

I'm ready for you, pockmark!

You'd like to kill me, eh gherkin? Scoffing braggart!

Saucy tramp! So you'd kill me, would you?...

There! Take that, centipede!

Oh, so you'd attack me from the rear, would you, cowards?...

Then look out for squalls!

Well, that's more or less what happened to my ancestor. As he hurled himself on the pirates, a heavy block dropped on his head, and he fell to the deck, stunned.

The pirates were masters of the ship. They had hoisted the red pennant - and they gave no quarter. Every man jack walked the plank ...

And Sir Francis?

Sir Francis? . . . When he came round he found himself securely lashed to his own mast. He suffered terribly . . .

From that blow on the head, of course . . .

No, from thirst! . . .

Poor man, how he suffered.

He looked about him. The deck was scrubbed, and no trace remained of the fearful combat that had taken place there. The pirates passed to and fro, each with a different load . . .

What's happening? Instead of pillaging our ship and making off with the booty, they're doing just the opposite.

But there's a man approaching. He wears a crimson cloak, embroidered with a skull: he's the pirate chief! He comes near - his breath reeks of rum - and he says:

Regard me well, dog: I am Red Rackham!

Your servant, sir. And I am Sir Francis Haddock.

Doesn't my name freeze your blood, eh? Right. Listen to me. You have killed Diego the Dreadful, my trusty mate. More than half my crew are dead or wounded. My ship is foundering, damaged by your first attack, then holed below the waterline as we boarded you . . .

. . . when some of your dastardly gunners fired at point blank range. She's sinking . . . so my men are transferring to this ship the booty we captured from a Spaniard three days ago.

And what booty!

Look at these diamonds!

These are worth more than six times a king's ransom . . .

Did you come here just to tell me that?

No, that's not why I came. I came to tell you that those who annoy me pay dearly for their folly! Tomorrow morning I shall hand you over to my crew. And that flock of lambs know just how to administer a lingering death!

So saying, he laughed sardonically, picked up his glass and drained it at a gulp, like this . . .

That's enough, Captain! Go on with your story . . .

Very well. Towards nightfall, the UNICORN with her pirate crew sighted a small island. Soon she dropped anchor in a sheltered cove . . .

Darkness fell; the pirates found the UNICORN's cargo of rum, broached the casks, and made themselves abominably drunk . . .

Abominably! . . . Yes abominably . . . that's the word . . .

Hey, what's the idea? . . . I only wanted to show you . . .

You don't have to, I quite understand.

Just as you like, Tintin . . . Now where was I?

The pirates were abominably drunk . . .

AAAAA-AAAAH!

?

That's funny! Now there are two glasses!

Well, in the meantime . . .

?

In the meantime Sir Francis struggled desperately to free himself . . .

Just you wait, my lambkins! Ration my rum if Sir Francis Haddock doesn't soon give you something to remember him by . . .

Done it! That's one hand free!

Free! Now I'm free!

On your guard, Red Rackham: here I come!

And with these words he hurled himself . . .

On the pirates? . . . Like that? . . . Unarmed? . . .

No, on a bottle of rum, rolling on the deck! . . . He opened it, put it to his lips, and . . .

And then he stops. "This is no time for drinking," he says, "I need all my wits about me." With that, he puts down the bottle . . .

Yes, he puts down the bottle . . . and seizes a cutlass. Then, looking towards the fo'c'sle where the drunken roistering still goes on . . .

You sing and carouse, little lambs! . . . I'm off to the magazine!

You know, of course, the magazine in a ship is where they store the gunpowder and shot . . .

There! . . . The party won't be complete without some fireworks!

Now I must make haste! There's just time for me to leave the ship before she goes up!

So, I've caught you!

!

So, dog, you'd blow us sky-high! . . . Well, you won't have that pleasure! I'll skin you alive, before I even douse that fuse!

By Lucifer! I'll shave your beard, porcupine!

And I'll pluck those feathers, squawking popinjay! Fancy-dress freebooter! Fresh water pirate! Pithecanthropus!

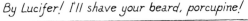

Retreat as you may, you cannot escape me!

I'll run you through, prattling porpoise!

24

And as he fought, Sir Francis kept thinking of that fuse, about to touch off the powder at any moment...

Suddenly, nimbly parrying a thrust, he leapt to one side...

With one swift blow from his heel he extinguished the fuse!

WOOOAH!

Now, Red Rackham, my temper's rising!

BANG ★ THUMP ★ ZZINNG ★ CRACK ★

Victory! Red Rackham lies dead! With a yo-ho-ho and a bottle of rum!

That's that! May heaven forgive your wicked soul!

Enough delay! Now to light another fuse...

...and be off!

No one has seen me: they're still drinking. Quick, into the jolly-boat...

Jusht look at the j-jolly-boat . . . Ish . . . ish going away . . .

Nonshensh! You're sheeing shings . . . you'sh drunk . . .

Hurrah! Justice is done!

So perished the UNICORN, that stout ship commanded by Sir Francis Haddock. And of all the pirates aboard her, not one escaped with his life . . .

What happened to Sir Francis after that?

He made friends with the natives on the island, and lived among them for two years. Then he was picked up by a ship which carried him back home. There his journal ends. But now comes the strangest thing in the whole story . . .

On the last page of the manuscript there is a sort of Will, in which he bequeaths to each of his three sons a model - built and rigged by himself - a model of the very ship he once blew up rather than leave her to the pirates. There's one funny detail: he tells his sons to move the mainmast slightly aft on each model. "Thus," he concludes, "the truth will out."

That's it, Captain! . . . Red Rackham's treasure will be ours!

What do you mean? Why do you suppose Sir Francis told his sons to move the mainmast on each of the three ships?

How should I know? He must have been a very particular man, and wanted the ships to be perfect!

In that case, he would have moved the masts himself. Why did he tell his sons to do it?

Because if his sons had obeyed him, they would have found a tiny scroll of parchment inside each mast!

What's that? How do you know?

Because I myself found the parchment hidden in the ship I bought in the Old Street Market. Here it is . . .

My wallet! . . . Someone's stolen my wallet . . .

Stolen it? You've probably left it at home.

No, it's been stolen. It was taken in the bus, on my way here. I remember being jostled . . .

What was on the parchment?

Wait . . . er . . . yes: *Three brothers joyned* - that's the three sons. *Three Unicorns in company sailing in the noonday Sunne will speak* - that means we must get the three ships to deliver their secret: the three parchments. The rest isn't so easy . . .

For 'tis from light that light will dawn. And then shines forth . . . and then some numbers, and at the end, a little cross follows the words *the Eagle's* . . . that's all.

But what can it mean?

I don't know yet, but I'm sure that if we can collect the three scrolls together, then we shall find Red Rackham's diamonds. I already know where the second one is. Come on, Captain!

You know where the second scroll is?

Yes, I know who's got the second UNICORN.

The second UNICORN built by my ancestor?

Yes, it belongs to a certain Mr Sakharine.

This is it: he lives here, at Number 21.

HELP! . . . HELP! . . . HELP! . . .

What's the matter? OOOH!...

Ooooh! Lord love us! It's Mr Sakharine... Someone's murdered Mr Sakharine!...

Dead?

No, he's alive: his heart's beating. He's been chloroformed...

Tintin, look there! The second UNICORN... and the mast's broken!

Look! The foot of the mast is hollow: the parchment has gone!

Thundering typhoons! We aren't the only ones hunting for Red Rackham's treasure!

Don't move, anyone!

Ah, my old friends! I...

I'm sorry. We're on duty. On duty we can have no friends!

Quite right! We're here to clear up this business...

First, here's the victim...

To be precise: here's the victim!

Now, if there's a victim, there must be a culprit.

A brilliant deduction! Now we only have to find him... and he can't be far away. To be precise: he isn't far away...

In fact, there he is!

Me, the culprit? You dare accuse me? ... Miserable earthworms! ... Sea gherkins!

Slave-traders! ... Sea-lice! ... Black-beetles! ... Baboons!

Artichokes! ... Vermicellis! ... Phylloxera! ... Pyrographers!

Crab-apples! ... Goosecaps! ... Gogglers! ... Jelly-fish!

Captain! Captain! Calm yourself!

Yes, please calm yourself, Captain. We only said that by way of an experiment ...

What sort of experiment?

You see, if you really had been guilty, you'd have been upset. As it is, we are now quite convinced of your innocence.

Now, to work! We must look for fingerprints.

Goodness gracious! ... The corpse has gone!

Look! ... Your corpse is coming round!

What happened to you, Mr Sakharine?

A man came here last night, to offer me some fine old engravings. As I bent over to look at them I felt a pad clamped over my nose ...

No doubt it was chloroform, for I became unconscious ...

Very odd ... To be precise ... Can you smell something burning?

Your magnifying-glass! Ha! ha! ha! . . . your magnifying-glass . . . and the sun! . . . Ha! ha! ha! . . .

Stop laughing in that stupid way! Try to concentrate on the case.

Can you describe the man who came to offer you those engravings?

Wait . . . I seem to have seen him before . . . but I can't tell where . . .

He was rather fat. Black hair, and a little black moustache. He wore a blue suit, and a brown hat.

That's him! . . . That's the man in the Old Street Market!

What man in the Old Street Market?

A man who tried to buy the ship I found in the Old Street Market. You know him too: he's the one you met on the stairs on your way to see me last night. You suspected him of stealing your wallet . . .

By the way, do you know mine has been stolen too? . . .

No! It's extraordinary how many people let their wallets be stolen! It's so easy not to . . . Here, you try and take mine . . .

Go on, try! . . .

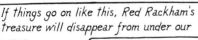

It's on elastic!

Simple enough . . . If you only think of it!

Childishly simple, in fact. But now we must leave you to your investigations. Goodbye . . .

Goodbye.

If things go on like this, Red Rackham's treasure will disappear from under our noses . . .

Yes, I'm afraid so . . .

Look, someone seems to be waiting for us outside my door . . .

The man from the Old Street Market!

Mr Tintin? . . .

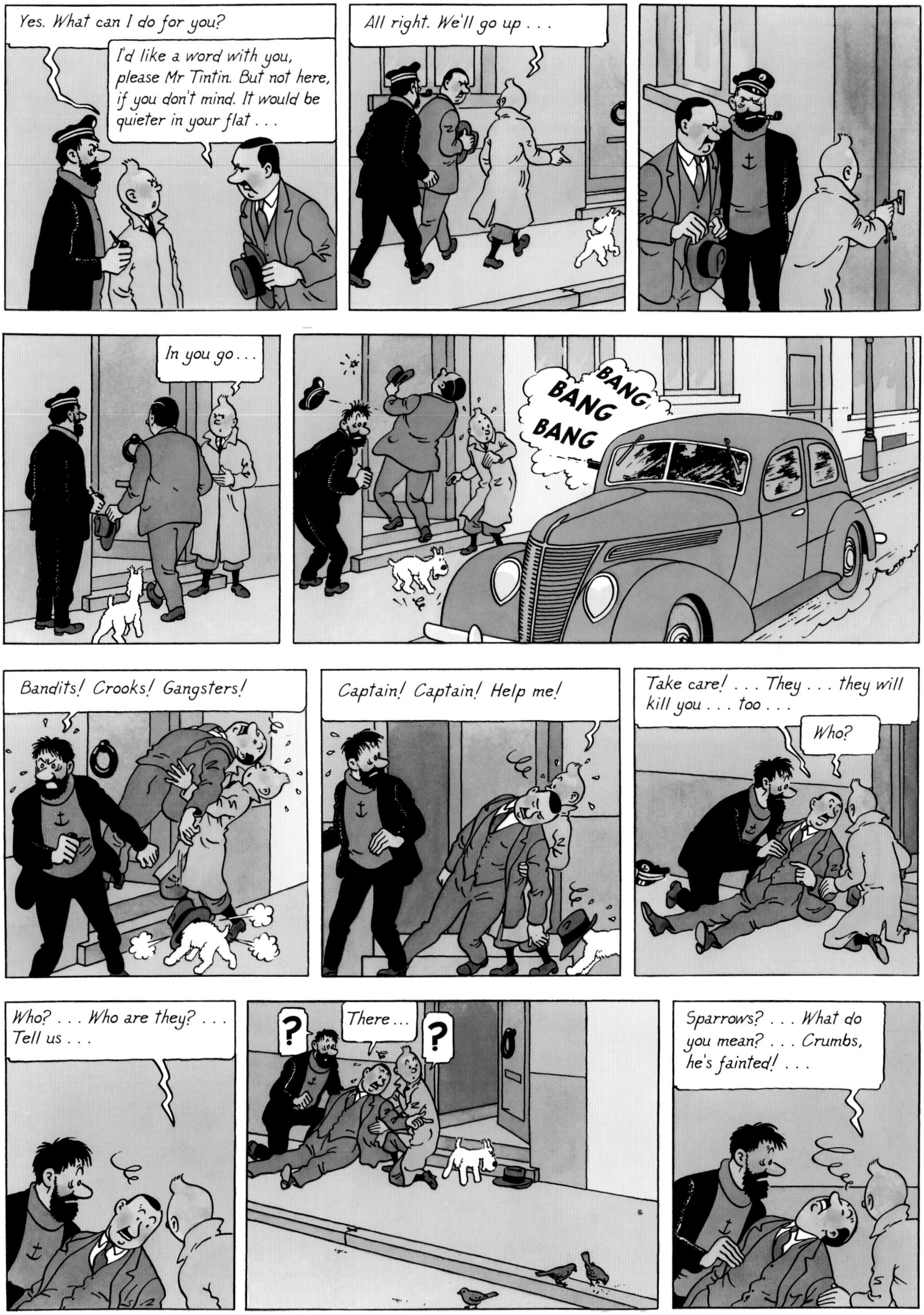
Yes. What can I do for you?
I'd like a word with you, please Mr Tintin. But not here, if you don't mind. It would be quieter in your flat . . .
All right. We'll go up . . .
In you go . . .
BANG
BANG
BANG
Bandits! Crooks! Gangsters!
Captain! Captain! Help me!
Take care! . . . They . . . they will kill you . . . too . . .
Who?
Who? . . . Who are they? . . . Tell us . . .
There . . .
?
?
Sparrows? . . . What do you mean? . . . Crumbs, he's fainted! . . .

Next morning...

SHOOTING DRAMA

AN unknown man was shot dead in Labrador Road just before midday yesterday. As he was about to enter No. 26, three shots were fired from a passing car which had slowed down opposite him. The victim was struck by all three bullets in the region of the heart. He died without regaining consciousness.

Poor devil. No one will ever know what he meant when he pointed to those sparrows.

Hello, Captain! Come in ... I'm just telephoning the hospital for news of the wounded man ...

It's no good: he's dead.

Hello? ... Is that the House-Surgeon? This is Tintin ... Good-morning, Doctor. How's our injured man? Just the same? Still unconscious? ... Is there any hope? A little ... yes ... Thank you. Goodbye.

But look here: it says in the paper that he's dead.

Yes, the papers were told he'd died. The crooks will believe he didn't give them away, so they won't be on their guard, and they'll get caught one day.

Ah, I see now. But I still wonder what that poor chap meant, pointing at those sparrows ...

So do I, Captain. It's all very mysterious. "To be precise: very mysterious", as the Thomsons would say.

Another day watching for pickpockets all over the place. I'll be glad to get back home.

Here comes our bus at last!

My wallet! ... This time I've got you, you scoundrel!

Stop, villain!

32

Ah, Captain! . . . Come with me . . .

Where? . . .

To see the Thomsons: they've found my wallet!

There's no mistake: it's mine all right.

He had seven in his pockets. The day's takings, no doubt.

Here's the parchment from the UNICORN's mast. Look, Captain . . .

Er . . . that's good . . .

Tell me: how did you manage to catch the thief?

Catch him? . . . Well, to be quite honest, we only managed to catch his morning-coat.

Yes, it's certainly a morning-coat. How odd for a pickpocket to wear a thing like this.

Isn't it?

The trouble is that the coat doesn't give us any clue about its owner's identity . . .

Doesn't it?

Look at these stitches; they make up a number. That means the coat has been to the cleaners recently.

Goodness, you're right!

So . . . to find the thief's name and address, we've only got to trace the cleaners who use this mark. Quick, we'll make a list of cleaners from the telephone directory, and start hunting for the thief at once!

CLEANERS

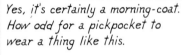

34

Some days later . . .

Mr Tintin?

The first   floor.

All right?   OK, OK.

Mr Tintin? Here's the dinner service you ordered.

Me? I haven't ordered anything.

But it's addressed to you . . . Look . . .

Right! The chloroform's done the trick. Quick, shove him in the crate.

Wait: I'll shut the door.

?

WOOAH! WOOAH!

Wasn't Mr Tintin in?

Yes, but there's some mistake. He hadn't   ordered anything.

That confounded tyke's at the window!

?

WOOAH! WOOAH!

Hello, Snowy! What's the matter?

Snowy! ... Snowy! ...
Be careful! You'll fall!

The dog's gone crazy: look at him chasing that van.

It's funny: he never leaves his master, as a rule.

Is Mr Tintin upstairs?

Yes, he's in.

Mrs Finch! ... Mrs Finch! ... Tintin isn't in his room!

Not in? ... Then where can he be?

Next morning . . .

Where on earth am I?

It looks very much as if I'm a prisoner . . .

Yes, a prisoner!

Two hours! . . . Two hours to get out of here! . . . How can I do it?

?

I wonder if I could use this beam as a battering-ram, against the door . . .

Hopeless! I can hardly lift it . . .

No good. But in two hours I must be miles away . . .

!

Eureka!

First I'd better block up this speaking tube with my hand-kerchief.

Then no one will hear any noise I may make . . .

Now to work! As fast as I can . . .

First I'll knot these sheets and blankets together . . .

Then tie them securely to this beam . . .

And pull! . . . Heave-ho! . . . Heave-ho! . . . Heave-ho! . . . Heave! . . .

Start again: I've simply got to move this beam. Now . . .

Meanwhile . . .

A quick bath and I'll soon get rid of this mud.

Aha! It's good to be nice and clean again.

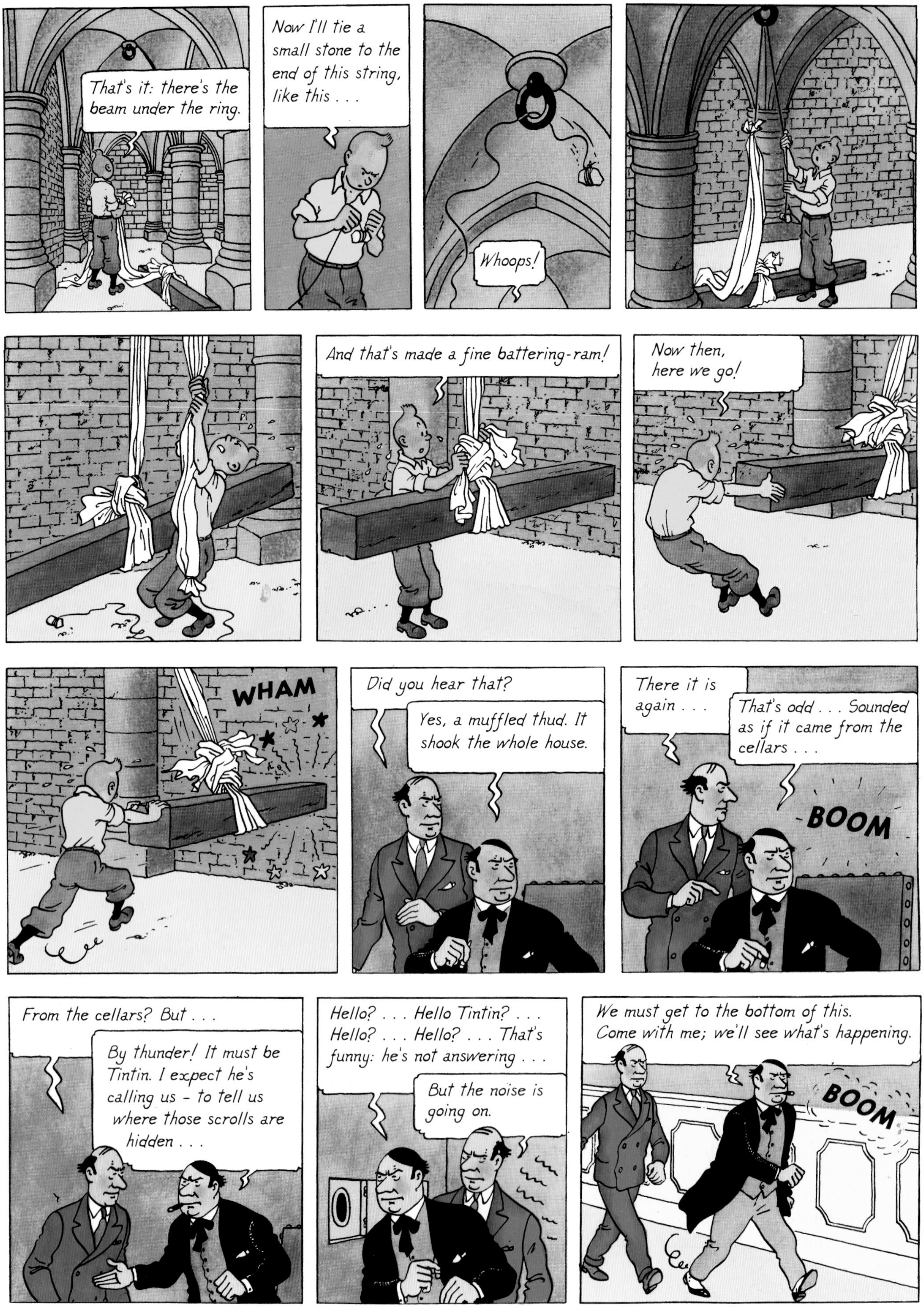
That's it: there's the beam under the ring.
Now I'll tie a small stone to the end of this string, like this . . .
Whoops!
And that's made a fine battering-ram!
Now then, here we go!
WHAM
Did you hear that?
Yes, a muffled thud. It shook the whole house.
There it is again . . .
That's odd . . . Sounded as if it came from the cellars . . .
BOOM
From the cellars? But . . .
By thunder! It must be Tintin. I expect he's calling us - to tell us where those scrolls are hidden . . .
Hello? . . . Hello Tintin? . . . Hello? . . . Hello? . . . That's funny: he's not answering . . .
But the noise is going on.
We must get to the bottom of this. Come with me; we'll see what's happening.
BOOM

It's coming from the cellars all right.

Now, one last go: the wall's cracked already, so . . .

Hooray, there she goes!

CRASH

?

!?

It's a musical-box! It fell over, and started to play!

There he is!

?

Over there . . . By thunder, he's rammed a hole through the wall!

Stop! . . . Stop! . . . Little devil, he's bolted!

See him? . . . There are plenty of hiding places here. But we'll get him.

Careful! We must be on our guard . . .

There! That armour . . . it moved!

!

So, my friend, you thought you'd be smart and hide in a suit of armour. Well, you're caught: come on out!

You won't? That's too bad for you! I'll count up to three and then I fire. One... two... three...

BANG

BANG

DONG

!

Confound it! He wasn't inside the armour!

Did you hear that?

Yes, it's nothing. A bullet ricocheted off the armour and struck that gong over there. Come on, don't let's waste time...

Whew! What luck! ... They've gone past. I'll just slip out...

Where are they? I can't see them...

CUCKOO!

CUCKOO!... CUCKOO! ... CUCKOO!

Stupid! That's not Tintin: it's a cuckoo-clock striking. Come, let's get on with it.

On you go, Tintin! You're in luck!

!

That was a good idea . . .

Little devil! He'll pay dearly for this . . .

So sorry to have to leave you, gentlemen . . .

And now, tough guys, it's your turn to be locked in . . .

No time to lose. I must have these gangsters arrested at once.

!

Now I see what he meant – the man who was shot – pointing to the birds. He was giving us the name of his attackers! . . . Just look at this letter . . .

Messrs. M. + G. Bird,
Antique Dealers,
Marlinspike Hall,
Marlinshire,
ENGLAND.

Quick, let's ring up the Captain . . .

Hello . . . yes . . . it's me . . . yes . . . Who's speaking? What? Tintin! . . . I . . . Where are you? Hello? . . . Hello? . . . Hello? . . . Hello? . . . Are you there? . . .

What am I doing here? . . . I . . . er . . . I'm Mr Bird's new secretary. Didn't you know that? . . .

I . . . no, I hadn't heard. Please excuse me, sir.

Hello, Nestor! . . . Nestor! . . .

Hello, Nestor! . . . A young ruffian's broken into the house! Stop him telephoning his accomplices! We're coming at once. Don't let him get away, whatever you do!

Hello, Captain! I'm at Marlinspike Hall . . . Bring the police! . . . What? . . . No, not in Greece – in Marlinspike Hall!

Drop that telephone, you!

Starlings bite? . . . Hello? . . . Hello? . . . Starlings bite what? . . .

Marlinspike, Captain! Marlinspike Hall!

What? . . . Martin's bike? . . . Hello? . . . Hello? . . . Thundering typhoons! What's going on?

Marlinspike Hall! . . . Marlinspike!

Hello, Captain? Can you hear me? . . . I'm at Marlinspike Hall! No, Marlinspike's the name!

What? . . . What sort of game? . . . Hello! He's rung off!

HELP! HELP!

That was Nestor's voice!

That's torn it! The telephone's broken!

There's only one thing to do - run for it - double quick!

If he's here he can't escape us . . .

46

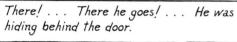

Go on, find him! We mustn't lose the scent.

Brutus! . . . Here Brutus!

WOOF! WOOF!

Saved! . . . What luck!

WOOF! WOOF!

WOOF! WOOF!

What shall I do? . . . If I run they'll let the dog go and I'll have them on my track. But if . . .

Yes, my mind's made up. I must risk everything!

We're nearly there; that barking isn't far off.

Whoops! That's it!

The joke's over, you gangsters! Hands up!

Now get up and start walking . . . Back to the house!

We can have a nice comfortable chat there while we wait for the police to arrive . . .

WOOF! WOOF!

CRACK

51

Where are they going? . . . Oh, I see: that little wretch is taking care to put Brutus back in his kennel.

WOOF! WOOF!

That's that! And now, gentlemen, we'll go to the police station!

They're coming back this way: they'll pass under the ground-floor windows. Perhaps there's some way . . .

Keep cool, Nestor!

Here they come! Careful, don't miss . . .

Nestor!

Oh, dear, I didn't hit him hard enough . . .

Now then, once more . . .

Oh dear!!

Got you this time, my young friend!

That's one for you, sycophant!

That thug had come round - he was just going to shoot you . . .

Let me go! . . . I keep telling you - it's all a mistake: I'm not the one to arrest . . .

Ah, here come Thomson and Thompson . . . Hello.

It's this little ruffian, this little wretch who broke into the house and terrorized my masters; he's a real gangster, Mr Detective . . .

It's true, Nestor acted in good faith. I heard his master say I was a criminal. Nestor believed it.

Then your masters are the criminals. Look what's left of my bottle of three-star brandy! It's all their fault! . . . They're gangsters! . . . dizzards! baboons!

And what's more, we have a warrant for their arrest.

My wallet! My wallet! It's incredible!

But your wallet's there . . .

That's just what's incredible: no one has stolen it!

By the way, what about that pickpocket? . . . Have you managed to lay hands on him?

Not yet, but it won't be long now.

We got his name from the Stellar Cleaners: he's called Aristides Silk. We were just about to pull him in when we were ordered to arrest the Bird brothers, and here we are . . .

Quiet! Quiet! Listen to me!

Gentlemen, there has been a miscarriage of justice! This man is innocent, as Tintin said. Won't you take off these handcuffs . . . and let him go and fetch me another bottle of brandy?

There, my man, now you're free. And we'll use these handcuffs for your masters!

We'll follow you, Nestor. Don't forget; it's to be three-star!

Now, Captain, tell me how you came to be here.

Oh, yes . . . Right. Well . . .

Just after your telephone call - and I didn't understand a word of that - someone rang up from the hospital . . .

. . . where they still had the little-birds-man. After hovering between life and death, he'd just come round and identified his attackers: the Bird brothers, antique dealers of Marlinspike Hall. It was only when I heard that name . . .

. . . that I understood what you meant on the telephone. There was no time to lose: I warned the police at once, and we rushed here . . .

WHAM* *OH! WHAM OW!

? ?

We shouldn't have left the police with those two gangsters! . . .

Look! . . . one's escaping! . . . there! He's just turned the corner!

He's the most dangerous of the two: he mustn't get away!

BRRRR BRRR

A car! That's a car starting up!

55

Road-hog! . . . Cyclone! . . . Bashi-bazouk! . . . Steamroller!

Too late! He's gone!

We'll take care of the other one later; let's go and help those two!

Wait: I'll give you a hand . . .

At last! . . . Got it!

Now, my friend, I'm waiting for an explanation . . .

I'm saying nothing!

Perhaps you don't know that your victim recovered yesterday, and divulged your name . . .

Our victim? I . . . Barnaby wasn't dead!

Very well: I'd better tell you everything. When we bought this house, two years ago, we found a little model ship in the attic, in very poor condition . . .

The UNICORN?

Yes, and when we were trying to restore the model we came across the parchment: its message intrigued us. My brother Max soon decided it referred to a treasure. But it spoke of three unicorns; so the first thing was to find the other two . . . You know we are antique dealers. We set to work . . .

. . . We used all our contacts: the people who comb the markets for interesting antiques; the people who hunt through attics; we told them to find the two ships. After some weeks one of our spies, a man called Barnaby, came and said he'd seen a similar ship in the Old Street Market. Unfortunately, this ship had just been sold to a young man; Barnaby tried in vain to buy it from him.

Yes, we know the rest. It was Barnaby whom you ordered to steal my UNICORN. But because the parchment wasn't there, he came back and ransacked the place – again unsuccessfully. And then?

Then? Oh well, I'd better tell you the lot . . .

Barnaby came back empty-handed. Then he suddenly remembered the other man who'd been trying to buy the ship from you.

And next day he visited Mr Sakharine, chloroformed him, and stole the third parchment . . .

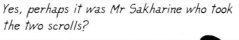

That's right. But after he'd given it to us, he and Max quarrelled violently about the money we'd agreed he should have. Barnaby demanded more, but Max stuck to the original sum. Finally Barnaby went, furiously angry and saying we'd regret our meanness. When he'd gone, Max got cold feet: supposing the wretch betrayed us? We jumped into the car and trailed him; our fears were justified. We saw him speaking . . .

. . . to you. Panicking in case he'd given the whole game away, Max caught up with you in a few seconds, and shot Barnaby as he stepped into your doorway.

I understand so far: but tell me, why did you kidnap me?

We told you: to make you give up the two parchments you had stolen from us a few days after the shooting.

I see. But I couldn't have stolen them as I didn't know you existed! But I wonder . . . Perhaps it was . . .

Yes, perhaps it was Mr Sakharine who took the two scrolls?

Hurrah! That's it!

At last! . . . He's managed to get it off for me . . .

Come on, Captain, we'd better help this poor chap . . .

Ready! Steady! He-e-eave!

Whoops!

Captain, as soon as we return we'll see Mr Sakharine. I'm sure he took the two scrolls . . .

Yes, we've only got one . . .

One! Great snakes! We haven't even got that! The Bird brothers took it! But we can get it back!

Give me back the parchment you stole from my room!

Give it back? . . . That's impossible . . . Max has it in his pocket!

!

Ring up the police-station at once; give them a description of Max Bird, and his car number – LX 188. Then we'll go straight back to town . . .

Right!

Next morning . . .

Now for Mr Sakharine . . .

RRRING

Mr Sakharine? He's gone away, young man. He won't be back for a fortnight.

He would be away! That doesn't make things any easier!

In the meantime I'll go and see the Thomsons. Perhaps they'll be able to tell me if they've found Max Bird . . .

Good morning. Are you going out? . . . I just came to ask you . . .

Sh! Mum's the word! Come with us!

Where are we going?

You'll soon see . . .

. . . and a few minutes later . . .

RAT TAT TAT TAT

Mr Aristides Silk?

Yes . . .

I arrest you in the name of the law!

Arrest me? . . .

Yes, you! You are a thief, sir! . . .

A thief! Aristides Silk, retired civil servant: a thief! It's a mistake, gentlemen, a shocking mistake!

I'm sorry to interrupt you, Mr Silk, but could you explain the meaning of all this? . . .

I . . . er, yes . . . Well, I . . . you see, I'm not a thief, certainly not! But I'm a bit of a . . . kleptomaniac. It's something stronger than I am: I adore wallets. So I . . . I . . . just find one from time to time. I put a label on it, with the owner's name . . .

. . . and I add it to my collection . . .

I venture to say, gentlemen, that this is a unique collection of its kind. And when I tell you that it only took me three months to assemble you'll agree that it's a remarkable achievement . . .

It's amazing! All these wallets in alphabetical order . . .

I wonder if by some extraordinary coincidence . . .

Hooray!

Property of: Max Bird pinched on 1 - 5 - 58

And here are the two pieces of parchment! . . . Captain, Red Rackham's treasure is ours!

Goodbye! Don't forget to have a look under the letter T!

Under letter T?

Look under T? Why under T? . . .

Good gracious! this belongs to me! . . .

"Property of Thompson"! This is yours! . . .

Property of Thomson . . . property of Thompson . . . Thomson . . . Thompson . . . Thomson . . . Thompson . . . Thomson . . . Thomson . . . Thompson . . . Thomson . . . Thomson . . . Thompson . . . Thompson . . .

Next day . . .

Red Rackham's treasure is ours: it's easy enough to say. We've found two of the scrolls, I know, but we still haven't got the third . . .

It looks as if . . .

RRRING
RRRING
RRRING

Hello? . . . Yes, it's me . . . Good morning . . . What? you've arrested him? . . .

Not exactly, but thanks to the clues we gave, they managed to catch him trying to leave the country . . .

What about the third parchment? . . . Did you find it on him? . . .

Yes, he had it. We're bringing it along to you. But first we've got a little account to settle with this troublesome antique dealer . . .

Here, Thompson, hold my stick while I just deal with this gentleman . . .

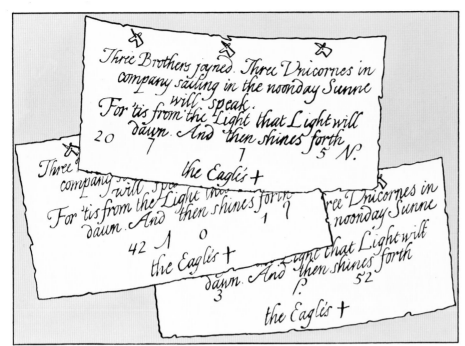

No! No! and No! You can go on hunting if you want to, but I've had enough: I give up. Blistering barnacles to that pirate Red Rackham, and his treasure! I'd sooner do without it; I'm not racking my brains any more trying to make sense out of that gibberish! Thundering typhoons! What a thirst it's given me!

I've got it, Captain! . . . I've got it! . . .

The message is right when it says that it is "from the light that light will dawn!" Look. I put them together . . .

. . . and hold them, "sailing in company", in front of the light. Look now! See what comes through! . . .

Thundering typhoons! The numbers and letters are completed,   and it gives us . . .

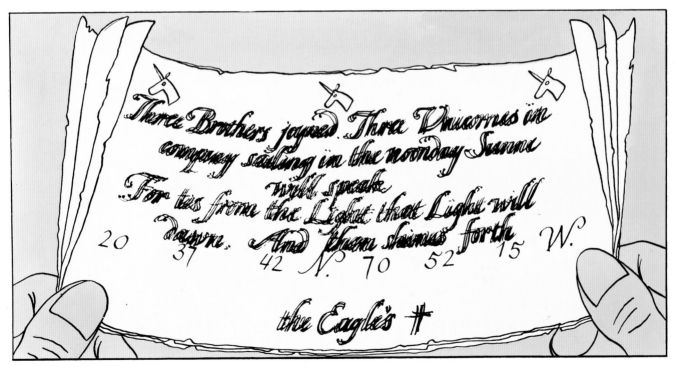

A latitude and a longitude!

Obviously telling us where the UNICORN sank!

Now, captain . . . When do we leave on our treasure-hunt?

When do we leave? . . . Er . . .

Let's see . . . first we need a ship . . . We can charter the SIRIUS, a trawler belonging to my friend, Captain Chester . . . Then we need a crew, some diving suits and all the right equipment for this sort of expedition . . . That will take us a little time to arrange. We'd better say a month. Yes, in a month we could be ready to leave.

Red Rackham's treasure will be ours!

But of course it won't be easy, and we shall certainly have plenty of adventures on our treasure-hunt . . . You can read about them in RED RACKHAM'S TREASURE!

- HERGÉ -